Usborne Dinosaur Tales

The Dinosaur
Who Stayed Indoors

Russell Punter

Illustrated by Andy Elkerton

Reading consultant: Alison Kelly

It's dawn in Dino Valley.
Most folk are out of bed...

like Sid

and Molly

Dot

and Spike.

But still not up is...
Fred.

Sid goes riding on his bike.

He visits his friend Fred.

"Let's go cycling,"
Sid shouts out.

But Fred stares
straight ahead.

Tuesday's hot.

So Fred's friend Dot
is heading to the bay.

"Let's go swimming, Fred!"
she calls.

But Fred shoos her away.

The next day – Wednesday – Spike goes by...

to soccer in the park.

"Join our match, Fred!"
Spike cries out.

But Fred stays in the dark.

"I'm watching cartoons on my phone. Please go away," he roars.

Come out to play!

Fred says...

NO WAY!

"I'd rather stay indoors."

By Friday, Fred is feeling bored.

He sees his friends online.

They're cycling...

16

swimming...

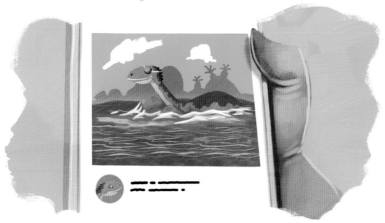

playing games...

and having a good time.

17

"Should I join them?"
wonders Fred.

Just then, Sid goes cycling by.

Come with me for a ride!

But Fred's spent so long
off his feet, his balance
is unsure.

He yelps for help
and wails...

OH NO!

"I think I'm best indoors."

21

Later he spots Dot.
"Hi Fred!"

It's such a lovely day!

"Why not join me
for a swim?"

They walk down
to the bay.

Fred's spent too long sitting down. His legs feel stiff and sore.

He moans and groans and sighs...

24

OH NO!

"I'll have to stay indoors."

Fred goes home
and sits alone.

Then Spike comes
round to call.

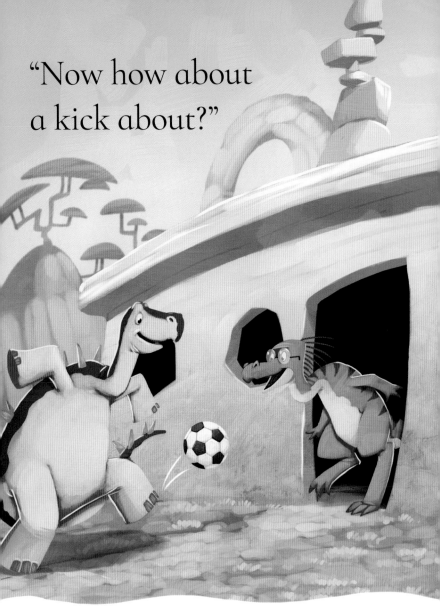

"Now how about
a kick about?"

Spike passes him the ball.

But Fred's been lazy for too long. "I'm tired out," he roars.

He huffs and puffs and gasps...

"I'll have to stay indoors."

29

Fred decides to exercise –
a little, every day.

And so he walks...

then jogs...

then runs...

until he feels okay.

Now he's fit to join
his friends.

He strides down
to the green.

"I'm feeling better," Fred declares. "Please may I join your team?"

Fred's really pleased
to be outdoors.

"Hey, I can play all day."

But then they hear
a cry of "Help!"

It's coming from the bay.

35

"Hang on, Molly!"
hollers Fred.

He grabs Sid's
mountain bike.

He cycles off,
down to the bay.

"Do hurry, Fred!"
yells Spike.

Fred is quick to reach
the beach.

He sprints across
the sand...

then dives into the
freezing sea...

and swims far out
from land.

Fred swims across
to Molly's boat.

"Climb on my back,"
he roars.

He makes his way through crashing waves.

Fred's friends are waiting on the beach.

Now Molly's safe and dry.

They gather round to say well done.

"You're really brave," they cry.

But after this, what will
Fred do? Will he stay in
once more?

Fred says...

NO WAY!

"I love to be outdoors!"

Series editor: Lesley Sims

First published in 2021 by Usborne Publishing Ltd., Usborne House,
83-85 Saffron Hill, London EC1N 8RT, England. usborne.com
Copyright © 2021 Usborne Publishing Ltd.

Look out for all the great stories in the Dinosaur Tales series!

Usborne Dinosaur Tales

The Dinosaur Who Lost His ROAR

Russell Punter
Illustrated by Andy Elkerton

Usborne Dinosaur Tales

The Dinosaur Who Roared For MORE

Russell Punter
Illustrated by Andy Elkerton